HARDLUCKY

HARDLUCKY

The Story of a Boy Who Learns How
to Think Before He Acts

Written by Miriam Chaikin

Illustrated by Gabriel Lisowski

Sky Pony Press
New York

Manufactured in China, July 2012
This product conforms to CPSIA 2008

Library of Congress Cataloging-in-Publication Data is available
on file.

ISBN: 978-1-61608-963-4

Graphic design by Michal Piekarski
Photography by Jerzy Malinowski

Dedicated to Samuel Chaikin Colman & Daniela Colman.
—M. C.

Dedicated to Miriam.
—G. L.

There once was a boy who forgot to pay attention to where he was or what he was doing. He walked into walls. He forgot to take his hand out of an open drawer before closing it. He often fell down stairs and sometimes even fell up them. And if there was something on the ground that other people stepped around, he always managed to step in it. People called him Hardlucky.

One day, while working for the wood cutter, Hardlucky left his cart on a hill and went to deliver wood. The cart slid downhill and hit a cow. The cow's owner got angry with the wood cutter, and the wood cutter, enraged, fired Hardlucky.

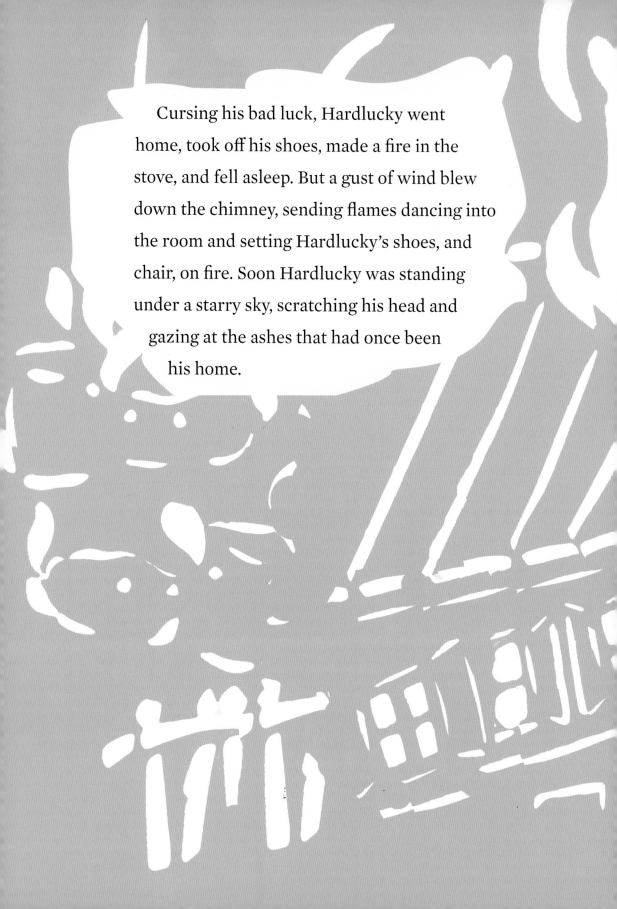

Cursing his bad luck, Hardlucky went home, took off his shoes, made a fire in the stove, and fell asleep. But a gust of wind blew down the chimney, sending flames dancing into the room and setting Hardlucky's shoes, and chair, on fire. Soon Hardlucky was standing under a starry sky, scratching his head and gazing at the ashes that had once been his home.

"Woe is me," Hardlucky wailed. "My hometown is bad luck for me."

So he decided to leave. He wrapped some stones in a bundle, so he could build a new house in a new town, and set out for the river.

There were two roads leading to the river. One was for travelers. The other—a shortcut—was very steep and used for goats. Hardlucky decided to take the shortcut but slipped and went tumbling down, his bundle bumping along after him all the way to the river. As he rolled down the hill, Hardlucky became tangled in his coat so he, too, looked like a bundle.

At the river, a ship's captain asked a sailor to bring him two forgotten bundles lying on the pier. But when the sailor did, the captain stood dumbfounded, watching one bundle uncurl itself and stand up—it was Hardlucky!

"Why have you disguised yourself as a bundle?" the captain asked.

Hardlucky stammered, trying to explain, but the captain thought he was just a stowaway.

"Liar!" the captain cried.

He gazed at the other bundle. "Get up, friend of a liar," he cried, giving the bundle a kick.

The captain broke his toe on the stones and
ordered Hardlucky to be arrested.

"Woe is me," Hardlucky moaned, sitting in the ship's jail. When the ship made a stop, two sailors grabbed him and flung him over the side, onto the ground. "Good riddance," they called after him.

Hardlucky got up and looked around. A group of people stood watching and one came walking toward him.

"A street urchin," Hardlucky thought.

"*Dja have nyk oinz,*" the man said, which in the language of the place meant "welcome."

Hardlucky thought the man had asked for some coins and so turned his pockets inside out, to show he had none.

"I'm sorry," Hardlucky said.

Once again, Hardlucky was thrown into jail, where he learned that in the language of the place, *ahm sah ri* meant, "I spit on your flag," and that the street urchin was actually an important citizen.

Hardlucky sat in jail, saying nothing and speaking to no one. In the morning, a guard took him to the border and shoved him over to the next town.

Hardlucky looked around and saw a sign that read: WELCOME TO KOTSK. Feeling sorry for himself, he sat down in the shade of a bush and began to wail: "Oh woe is me, Woe! Woe!"

A horse pulling a cart and its driver heard Hardlucky cry, "Woe!" and came to a stop. The driver got down and approached Hardlucky.

"Why are you so unhappy?" he asked.

Hardlucky looked up. It had been so long since anyone had spoken kindly to him that he began to cry. And through his tears, he told his unlucky story.

The driver smiled. "You are in Kotsk. Our rabbi will help you," he said.

And then Hardlucky remembered. He had heard stories about the wise rabbi of Kotsk.

The driver pointed and said, "That's the rabbi's house, there on the hill." Hardlucky climbed the hill, feeling hopeful. He knocked on the door and was let into a room to wait with many others. Finally, the rabbi sent for him.

"Speak," said the rabbi.

Between tears, Hardlucky told his story.

The rabbi smiled.

"Now I will speak. Don't answer—just listen. If you had put a stick under the wheel of the cart, would it have rolled downhill?"

"I—" Hardlucky began.

"I said, just listen," the rabbi interrupted. "If you had put your shoes further from the flames, would they have caught fire? If you had taken the normal road to the river, would you have fallen and been mistaken for a bundle? As for the stones, why carry them from place to place? There are stones everywhere!"

Hardlucky was beginning to understand.

"As for that street urchin," the rabbi continued, "if you had paid attention, you would have seen that the urchin was important and noticed that he was speaking a different language."

Hardlucky smiled. "Then I'm not unlucky?"

"No, just a bit . . . slow," said the rabbi. "But if you pay attention and stop to think before you act, you will see how your luck will change."

Hardlucky got up to leave. "Thank you, rabbi," he said, bowing and walking backwards to the door, as a sign of respect.

Once outside, happiness washed over him, and he began to run, jump, and skip. Then he tripped and fell.

As he picked himself up he saw a sign that read: Do Not Run, Jump, or Skip.

"I must start paying attention," he said.

Hardlucky decided to return home. "My town is innocent," he thought. "I caused my own bad luck."

With the rabbi's words dancing in his head, he walked to the pier—keeping away from doors, looking straight ahead, and stepping around anything on the ground that should be avoided.

At the port, he found a ship going to his hometown and asked for work.

"What can you do?" the captain asked.

Hardlucky was going to answer "nothing," but stopped to think. If he said nothing, he would get nothing.

"I can do anything if someone shows me how," he finally said.

So, the captain sent him to help the cook. The cook taught him to crack an egg on the side of a dish. Hardlucky paid close attention and learned to make scrambled eggs and sunny-side-up eggs and omelets.

Determined to succeed, he memorized the steps: "Crack, beat, add salt, mix, drop into pan, watch, turn, watch, remove from the flame."

When Hardlucky left the ship, the captain gave him a hen as a parting gift. The crew gave him a frying pan.

Everyone in the village was happy to see Hardlucky return. They all helped him get settled in. The wood cutter gave him wood to rebuild his house. Outside, with some rocks, he built a fireplace for cooking. He turned an old wooden crate on its side and called it a table. And he hung up a sign reading HARDLUCKY'S OMELETS. Before the day was out, he had a place to live and was the owner of a restaurant.

News of the restaurant spread, and people came from all over to sample Hardlucky's omelets.

Their favorites were the garlic omelet he
named *Think*, the one with herring he called
Look, and the one with onions he called *Listen*.

At first, people found the names peculiar. But they soon realized the omelets were delicious and Think, Look, and Listen rang through the air as Hardlucky and his assistant—yes, he now had an assistant—hurried to satisfy their customers.

People still called him Hardlucky, but no one could remember why—not even Hardlucky himself. Each night, he fell asleep with a smile on his lips, thinking of the Kotsker rabbi and all the good luck he now had.

HISTORICAL NOTE
BY GABRIEL LISOWSKI

Almost two hundred years ago, in Eastern Europe, communities of Hasidim—Jewish thinkers and mystics—thrived. They were the heirs to three thousand years of Jewish tradition and religion. Hasidim were deeply religious Jews who devoted themselves to following the teachings of Torah, to study, and to help the poor.

A *tzadik*, meaning "the righteous one," was the holiest among them. He was seen as a true intermediary between God and a person.

Kotsker Rebbe was such a *tzadik*. He lived from 1787 until 1859. On holy days, he held court.

Thousands of Jews came to bask in his presence and to seek his advice.

One day, he withdrew from the outside world for twenty years, in order to study the Torah and write in solitude. At the end of each year, he burned his writings. Fortunately, many of his proverbs and sayings were written down by his disciples to preserve them for future generations.

My grandmother often told me tales about our ancestor, the Kotsker Rebbe, and at the end of each tale, she would say, "Never forgot to honor the memory of this holy man."